'This is as much a mystery as the Immaculate Conception, which of itself must make a doctor an unbeliever.'

D0417923

HONORÉ DE BALZAC
Born 1799, Tours, France
Died 1850, Paris

'The Atheist's Mass' and 'The Conscript' were first published
in their original French in 1836 and 1831 respectively.
They are taken from *Selected Short Stories*.

BALZAC IN PENGUIN CLASSICS

HONORÉ DE BALZAC

The Atheist's Mass

Translated by
Sylvia Raphael

PENGUIN BOOKS

PENGUIN CLASSICS

Published by the Penguin Group
Penguin Books Ltd, 80 Strand, London WC2R ORL, England
Penguin Group (USA) Inc., 375 Hudson Street, New York, New York 10014, USA
Penguin Group (Canada), 90 Eglinton Avenue East, Suite 700, Toronto, Ontario,
Canada M4P 2Y3 (a division of Pearson Penguin Canada Inc.)
Penguin Ireland, 25 St Stephen's Green, Dublin 2, Ireland
(a division of Penguin Books Ltd)
Penguin Group (Australia), 707 Collins Street, Melbourne, Victoria 3008, Australia
(a division of Pearson Australia Group Pty Ltd)
Penguin Books India Pvt Ltd, 11 Community Centre, Panchsheel Park,
New Delhi – 110 017, India
Penguin Group (NZ), 67 Apollo Drive, Rosedale, Auckland 0632, New Zealand
(a division of Pearson New Zealand Ltd)
Penguin Books (South Africa) (Pty) Ltd, Block D, Rosebank Office Park,
181 Jan Smuts Avenue, Parktown North, Gauteng 2193, South Africa

Penguin Books Ltd, Registered Offices: 80 Strand, London WC2R ORL, England

www.penguin.com

This edition published in Penguin Classics 2015
001

Translation copyright © Sylvia Raphael, 1977

The moral right of the translator has been asserted

Set in 9.5/13 pt Baskerville 10 Pro
Typeset by Jouve (UK), Milton Keynes
Printed in Great Britain by Clays Ltd, St Ives plc

A CIP catalogue record for this book is available from the British Library

ISBN: 978-0-141-39742-9

www.greenpenguin.co.uk

Contents

The Atheist's Mass

A doctor to whom science owes a fine physiological theory and who, while still young, achieved a place amongst the celebrities of the Paris school of medicine (that centre of enlightenment to which all the doctors of Europe pay homage), Doctor Bianchon, practised surgery for a long time before devoting himself to medicine. His early studies were directed by one of the greatest of French surgeons, by the celebrated Desplein who passed through the world of science like a meteor. Even his enemies admit that he took with him to the grave a method that could not be handed on to others. Like all men of genius he had no heirs; he carried his skill within him and he carried it away with him. A surgeon's fame is like an actor's. It exists only so long as he is alive and his talent can no longer be appreciated once he has gone. Actors and surgeons, great singers too, and virtuoso musicians who by their playing increase tenfold the power of music, are all heroes of the moment. Desplein's life is a proof of the resemblance between the destinies of these transitory geniuses. His name which was so famous yesterday is almost forgotten today. It will remain only in his own field without going beyond it. But extraordinary

1

conditions are surely necessary for the name of a scholar to pass from the domain of Science into the general history of humanity. Did Desplein have that width of knowledge which makes a man the mouthpiece or the representative of an age? Desplein possessed a god-like glance; he understood the patient and his disease by means of a natural or acquired intuition which allowed him to appreciate the diagnosis appropriate to the individual, to decide the precise moment, the hour, the minute at which he should operate, taking into account atmospheric conditions and temperamental peculiarities. To be able to collaborate with Nature in this way, had he then studied the endless combination of beings and elemental substances contained in the atmosphere or provided by the earth for man, who absorbs them and uses them for a particular purpose? Did he use that power of deduction and analogy to which Cuvier owes his genius? However that may be, this man understood the secrets of the flesh; he understood its past as well as its future, by studying the present. But did he contain all science in his person as did Hippocrates, Galen, Aristotle? Did he lead a whole school towards new worlds? No. If it is impossible to refuse to this constant observer of human chemistry the ancient science of Magism, that is to say, the knowledge of the elements in fusion, of the causes of life, of life before life, of what it will be, judging from its antecedents before it exists, all this unfortunately was personal to him. In his life he was isolated by egoism, and today that egoism is the death of his fame. Over his tomb there is no statue proclaiming to the future, in ringing tones, the mysteries which Genius seeks out at its own expense. But perhaps Desplein's talent was in keeping with his beliefs, and consequently mortal. For him the terrestrial atmosphere was like a generative bag; he saw the earth as if it were an egg in its shell, and unable to know whether the egg or the hen came first, he denied both the fowl and the egg. He believed neither in the animal anterior to man nor in the spirit beyond him. Desplein was not in doubt, he affirmed his opinion. He was like many other scholars in his frank, unmixed atheism. They are the best people in the world but incorrigible atheists, atheists such as religious people don't believe exist. It was hardly possible for such a man to hold a different opinion, for from his youth he was used to dissecting the living being *par excellence*, before, during and after life, and to examining all its functions without finding the unique soul that is indispensable to religious theories. Desplein recognized a cerebral centre, a nervous centre and a circulatory centre, of which the first two do duty for each other so well that at the end of his life he was convinced that the sense of hearing was not absolutely necessary to hear, nor the sense of sight absolutely necessary to see, and that the solar plexus could replace them without anyone noticing it. He thus found two souls in man and this fact confirmed his atheism, although it still tells us nothing about God. He died, they say, impenitent to the

3

last, as unfortunately do many fine geniuses. May God forgive them!

This really great man's life exhibited many pettinesses, to use the expression of his enemies who in their jealousy wanted to diminish his fame, but it would be more appropriate to call them apparent contradictions. Envious or stupid people who do not know the reasons which explain the activities of superior minds immediately take advantage of a few superficial contradictions to make accusations on which they obtain a momentary judgement. If, later on, the plans which have been attacked are crowned with success, when the preparations are correlated with the results, some of the calumnies which were made beforehand remain. Thus, in our own time, Napoleon was condemned by our contemporaries when he spread out the wings of his eagle over England: but we needed the events of 1822 to explain 1804 and the flat-bottomed boats at Boulogne.*

Since Desplein's fame and scientific knowledge were unassailable, his enemies attacked his strange disposition and his character, while in fact he was simply what the English call eccentric. At times he dressed magnificently

---

* In 1804 Napoleon planned to invade England, using a fleet of flat-bottomed boats based on Boulogne. But he was unable to gain command of the sea, and abandoned this plan in favour of the land conquest of Europe. In 1822 the French Government wanted to intervene in the civil conflict in Spain, in spite of the vigorous protest of Great Britain. Balzac's point is, however, unclear.

like the tragedian Crébillon, at times he seemed unusually indifferent to clothes. Sometimes he was to be seen in a carriage, sometimes on foot. He was now sharp-tempered, now kind, apparently hard and stingy, yet capable of offering his fortune to his exiled rulers who honoured him by accepting it for a few days. No man has inspired more contradictory judgements. Although, to obtain the Order of Saint Michael (which doctors are not supposed to solicit), he was capable of dropping a Book of Hours from his pocket at Court, you can be sure that inwardly he laughed at the whole thing. He had a profound con-tempt for mankind, having studied them from above and from below, having surprised them without pretence, as they performed the most solemn as well as the pettiest acts of life. A great man's gifts often hang together. If one of these giants has more talent than wit, his wit is still greater than that of a man of whom one says simply, 'He is witty.' All genius presupposes moral insight. This insight may be applied to some speciality, but he who sees the flower must see the sun. The doctor who heard a diplomat whose life he had saved ask, 'How is the Emperor?', and who replied, 'The courtier is coming back to life, the man will follow!' was not only a surgeon or a physician, he was also extremely witty. Thus the close and patient observer of humanity will justify Desplein's exor-bitant pretensions and will realize, as he himself realized, that he was capable of being as great a minister as he was a surgeon.

Among the riddles which Desplein's life reveals to his contemporaries we have chosen one of the most interesting, because the solution will be found at the end of this tale and will answer some of the foolish accusations which have been made against him.

Of all the pupils whom Desplein had at his hospital, Horace Bianchon was one of those to whom he became most warmly attached. Before doing his internship at the Hôtel Dieu,* Horace Bianchon was a medical student, living in a miserable boarding-house in the Latin Quarter, known by the name of La Maison Vauquer.† There this poor young man experienced that desperate poverty which is a kind of melting-pot whence great talents emerge pure and incorruptible, just as diamonds can be subjected to any kind of shock without breaking. In the violence of their unleashed passions, they acquire the most unshakeable honesty, and by dint of the constant labour with which they have contained their balked appetites, they become used to the struggles which are the lot of genius. Horace was an upright young man, incapable of double-dealing in affairs of honour, going straight to the point without fuss, as capable of pawning his coat for his friends as of giving them his time and his night's rest.

---

* L'Hôtel-Dieu was one of the oldest and most important hospitals in Paris.
† Life in La Maison Vauquer is depicted in Balzac's novel *Le Père Goriot.*

In short, Horace was one of those friends who are not worried about what they receive in exchange for what they give, certain as they are to receive in their turn more than they will give. Most of his friends had for him that inner respect which is inspired by unostentatious goodness, and several of them were afraid of his strictures. But Horace exercised these virtues without being prudish. He was neither a puritan nor a preacher; he swore quite readily when giving advice, and enjoyed a good meal in gay company when opportunity offered. He was good company, no more squeamish than a soldier, bluff and open, not like a sailor – for the sailor of today is a wily diplomatist – but like a fine young man who has nothing to hide in his life; he walked with his head high and his heart light. In a word, Horace was the Pylades of more than one Orestes, creditors being today the most real shape assumed by the ancient Furies. He wore his poverty with that gaiety which is perhaps one of the greatest elements of courage, and like all those who have nothing, he contracted few debts. Sober as a camel, brisk as a stag, he was unwavering both in his principles and in his behaviour. The happiness of Bianchon's life began on the day when the famous surgeon obtained evidence of the good qualities and failings which, the one as much as the other, made Doctor Horace Bianchon doubly precious to his friends. When a clinical chief adopts a young man, that young man has, as they say, his foot in the stirrup. Desplein always took Bianchon with him to act as his assistant in well-to-do homes, where

7

some reward would nearly always find its way into the student's purse, and where little by little the mysteries of Parisian life were revealed to the young provincial. Desplein also kept him in his surgery during consultations and gave him work to do there. Sometimes he would send him to accompany a rich patient to a spa. In short, he was making a practice for him. The result of all this was that after a time the lord of surgery had a devoted slave. These two men, the one at the height of his fame and leader of his profession, enjoying an immense fortune and an immense reputation, the other, a modest Omega, having neither fortune nor fame, became intimate friends. The great Desplein told his assistant everything. He knew if a certain lady had sat down on a chair beside the master, or on the famous surgery couch where Desplein slept. Bianchon knew the mysteries of that temperament, both lion-like and bull-like, which in the end expanded and abnormally developed the great man's chest and caused his death from enlargement of the heart. The student studied the eccentricities of Desplein's very busy life, the plans made by his sordid avarice, the hopes of the politician concealed behind the scientist; he foresaw the disappointments in store for the only feeling hidden in that heart which was hardened rather than hard.

One day Bianchon told Desplein that a poor water-carrier from the Saint-Jacques quarter had a horrible illness caused by fatigue and poverty; this poor Auvergnat had eaten only potatoes during the severe winter of 1821. Desplein left all his patients. At the risk of working his horse to death, he rode as fast as he could, followed by Bianchon, to the poor man's house and himself had him carried to the nursing-home founded by the famous Dubois in the Faubourg Saint-Denis. Desplein attended the man, and when he had cured him, gave him the money to buy a horse and a water-cart. This Auvergnat was remarkable for one original characteristic. One of his friends fell ill; he took him straight away to Desplein and said to his benefactor, 'I would not have allowed him to go to another doctor.' Surly as he was, Desplein grasped the water-carrier's hand and said, 'Bring them all to me.' And he had the peasant from the Cantal admitted to the Hôtel Dieu, where he took the greatest care of him. Bianchon had already noticed several times that his chief had a predilection for Auvergnats, and especially for water-carriers. But as Desplein had a kind of pride in his treatments at the Hôtel Dieu, his pupil didn't see anything very strange in that.

One day, as Bianchon was crossing the Place Saint-Sulpice, he noticed his master going into the church about nine o'clock in the morning. Desplein, who at that period of his life never moved a step except by carriage, was on foot and slipping in by the door of the Rue du Petit-Lion, as if he had been going into a house of doubtful reputation. Bianchon's curiosity was naturally aroused, since he knew his master's opinions and that he was a 'devyl' of a Cabanist* (devyl with a y, which in Rabelais seems to suggest a superiority in devilry). Slipping into Saint-Sulpice, he was not a little astonished to see the great Desplein, that atheist without pity for the angels, who cannot be subjected to the surgeon's knife, who cannot have sinus or gastric trouble, that dauntless scoffer, kneeling humbly, and where? . . . in the chapel of the Virgin, where he listened to a Mass, paid for the cost of the service, gave alms for the poor, all as solemnly as if he had been performing an operation.

'He certainly didn't come to clear up questions about the Virgin birth,' said Bianchon in boundless astonishment. 'If I had seen him holding one of the tassels of the canopy on Corpus Christi day, I would have taken it as a joke; but at this hour, alone, with no one to see him, that certainly gives one food for thought!'

Bianchon did not want to look as if he was spying on the chief surgeon of the Hôtel Dieu and he went away. By chance Desplein invited him to dinner that very day, not at home but at a restaurant.

Between the fruit and the cheese, Bianchon managed skilfully to bring the conversation round to the subject of the Mass, calling it a masquerade and a farce.

'A farce,' said Desplein, 'which has cost Christendom

---

* Cabanis was the author of the *Traité du physique et du moral de l'homme*, an influential atheistic and materialistic work.

more blood than all Napoleon's battles and all Broussais' leeches! The Mass is a papal invention which goes no further back than the sixth century and which is based on *Hoc est corpus*. What torrents of blood had to be spilt to establish Corpus Christi day! By the institution of this Feast the court of Rome intended to proclaim its victory in the matter of the Real Presence, a schism which troubled the Church for three centuries. The wars of the Counts of Toulouse and the Albigensians are the tail-end of this affair. The Vaudois and the Albigensians* refused to recognize this innovation.'

In short Desplein enjoyed himself, giving free rein to his atheistic wit, and pouring out a flood of Voltairean jokes, or, to be more precise, a horrible parody of the *Citateur*.†

'Well,' Bianchon said to himself, 'where is the pious man I saw this morning?'

He said nothing; he had doubts whether he really had seen his chief at Saint-Sulpice. Desplein would not have bothered to lie to Bianchon. They both knew each other too well; they had already exchanged ideas on subjects which were just as serious, and they had discussed systems *de natura rerum*, probing or dissecting them with the knives and the scalpel of incredulity. Three months went

---

* The Vaudois and the Albigensians were twelfth-century heretical sects in the south of France.

† *Le Citateur* was an anti-clerical pamphlet by Pigault-Lebrun.

by. Bianchon did not follow up the incident, although it remained stamped on his memory. One day in the course of that year, one of the doctors at the Hôtel Dieu took Desplein by the arm, in Bianchon's presence, as if to ask him a question.

'What were you going to do at Saint-Sulpice, my dear chief?' he asked.

'I went to see a priest who had a diseased knee. Madame la Duchesse d'Angoulême did me the honour of recommending me,' said Desplein.

The doctor was satisfied with this excuse, but not so Bianchon.

'Oh! So he goes to see bad knees in church! He was going to hear Mass,' the student said to himself.

Bianchon determined to keep a watch on Desplein. He recalled the day and the time on which he had surprised him going in to Saint-Sulpice and he determined to go there the following year on the same day and at the same time, to find out if he would surprise him there again. If that happened, the regularity of his worship would justify a scientific investigation, for in such a man there should not be a direct contradiction between thought and deed. The following year, on the day and at the hour in question, Bianchon, who was by this time no longer Desplein's assistant, saw the surgeon's carriage stop at the corner of the Rue de Tournon and the Rue du Petit-Lion. From there his friend crept stealthily along by the walls of Saint-Sulpice where he again heard Mass at the altar of the Virgin. It was certainly Desplein, the chief surgeon, the atheist *in petto*, the pious man on occasion. The plot became more involved. The famous scientist's persistence complicated everything. When Desplein had left the church, Bianchon went up to the sacristan who came to minister to the chapel, and asked him if the gentleman was a regular attendant.

'I have been here for twenty years,' said the sacristan, 'and for all that time Monsieur Desplein has been coming four times a year to hear this Mass; it was he who founded it.'

'*He* founded it!' said Bianchon as he walked away. 'This is as much a mystery as the Immaculate Conception, which of itself must make a doctor an unbeliever.'

Although Dr Bianchon was a friend of Desplein's, some time went by before he was in a position to speak to him about this strange circumstance of his life. If they met at a consultation or in society, it was difficult to find that moment of confidence and solitude when, with feet up on the fire-dogs and heads leaning against the backs of their chairs, two men tell each other their secrets. Finally, seven years later, after the 1830 Revolution, when the people stormed the Archbishopric, when, inspired by Republican sentiments, they destroyed the golden crosses which appeared, like flashes of lightning, in this vast sea of houses, when Disbelief and Violence swaggered together through the streets, Bianchon surprised Desplein going into Saint-Sulpice. The doctor followed him in and took a place near him without his friend making the least sign or showing the least surprise. Both of them heard the foundation Mass.

'Will you tell me, my friend,' Bianchon said to Desplein when they were outside the church, 'the reason for this display of piety? I have already caught you three times going to Mass, you! You must tell me the reason for this mysterious activity, and explain to me the flagrant discrepancy between your opinions and your behaviour. You don't believe in God, yet you go to Mass! My dear chief, you must answer me.'

'I am like many pious men, men who appear to be profoundly religious but are quite as atheistic as we are, you and I.'

And he let forth a torrent of epigrams about political personalities of whom the best known provides us in this century with a new edition of Molière's Tartuffe.

'That's not what I am talking about,' said Bianchon. 'I want to know the reason for what you have just been doing here. Why did you found this Mass?'

'Well, my dear friend,' said Desplein, 'since I am on the brink of the grave, there is no reason why I shouldn't speak to you about the beginning of my life.'

At this moment Bianchon and the great man happened to be in the Rue des Quatre-Vents, one of the most horrible streets in Paris. Desplein pointed to the sixth storey of one of those houses which are shaped like an obelisk and have a medium-sized door opening on to a passage.

At the end of the passage is a spiral staircase lit by apertures called *jours de souffrance*. The house was a greenish colour; on the ground floor lived a furniture dealer; a different kind of poverty seemed to lodge on each floor. Raising his arm with an emphatic gesture, Desplein said to Bianchon, 'I lived up there for two years.'

'I know the place; d'Arthez lived there and I came here almost every day in my youth. At that time we called it the "jar of great men"! Well, what of it?'

'The Mass that I have just heard is linked to events which took place at the time when I lived in the attic where, so you tell me, d'Arthez lived. It is the one where a line of washing is dangling at the window above a pot of flowers. I had such a difficult time to start with, my dear Bianchon, that I can dispute the palm of the sufferings of Paris with anyone. I have put up with everything, hunger, thirst, lack of money, lack of clothes, of footwear, of linen, everything that is hardest about poverty. I have blown on my numbed fingers in that "jar of great men" which I should like to visit again with you. I worked during one winter, when I could see my own head steaming and a cloud of my own breath rising like horses' breath on a frosty day. I don't know what enables a man to stand up to such a life. I was alone, without help, without a farthing either to buy books or to pay the expenses of my medical education. I had no friends and my irritable, sensitive, restless temperament did me no good. No one could see that my bad temper was caused by the difficulties and the work of a man who, from his position at the bottom of the social ladder, was striving to reach the top. But I can tell *you*, you to whom I don't need to pretend, that I had that basis of good feeling and keen sensitivity which will always be the prerogative of men who, after having been stuck for a long time in the slough of poverty, are strong enough to climb to any kind of summit. I could get nothing from my family or my home beyond the inadequate allowance they made me. In short, at this period of my life, all I had to eat in the mornings was a roll which the baker in the Rue du Petit-Lion sold me more cheaply because it was yesterday's, or the day before yesterday's. I crumbled it up into some milk and so my morning meal cost me only two sous. I dined only every other day at a boarding-house where dinner cost sixteen sous. In this way I spent only nine sous a day. You know as well as I do the care I had to take of my clothes and my footwear. I don't think, later on in life, we are as much distressed by a colleague's disloyalty as you and I were when we saw the mocking grin of a shoe that was becoming unsewn, or heard the armhole of a frock-coat split. I drank only water; I had the greatest respect for cafés. Zoppi's seemed to me like a promised land which the Luculli of the Latin Quarter alone had the right to patronize. Sometimes I wondered whether I would ever be able to have a cup of white coffee there, or play a game of dominoes. In short, I transferred to my work the fury which poverty inspired in me. I tried to master scientific

knowledge so that I should have an immense personal
worth deserving of the place I would reach when I
emerged from my obscurity. I consumed more oil than
bread; the light which lit up those stubborn vigils cost
me more than my food. The struggle was long, hard and
unrelieved. I aroused no feelings of friendship in those
around me. To make friends, you must mix with young
people, have a few sous so that you can go and have
a drink with them, go with them everywhere where stu-
dents go. I had nothing. And no one in Paris realizes that
"nothing" is "nothing". When there was any question of
revealing my poverty I experienced that nervous contrac-
tion of the throat which makes our patients think that a
ball is rising up from the gullet into the larynx. Later on
I met people who, born rich and never having lacked for
anything, don't know the problem of this rule of three:
"A young man is to crime as a hundred sous piece is to X."
These gilded fools say to me, "Why did you get into debt?
Why did you take on such crushing obligations?" They
remind me of the princess who, knowing that the people
were dying of hunger, asked, "Why don't they buy cake?"
I should very much like to see one of those rich people,
who complains that I charge too much for operating on
him, alone in Paris, without a penny, without a friend,
without credit and forced to work with his two hands to
live. What would he do? Where would he satisfy his
hunger? Bianchon, if at times you have seen me bitter
and hard, it was because I was superimposing my early

sufferings on the lack of feeling, the selfishness, of which I had thousands of examples in high places; or I was thinking of the obstacles which hatred, envy, jealousy, and calumny have placed between me and success. In Paris, when certain people see you ready to put your foot in the stirrup, some of them pull you back by the coat-tail, others loosen the buckle of the saddle-girth so that you'll fall and break your head; this one takes the shoes of your horse, that one steals your whip. The least treacherous is the one you see coming up to shoot you at point-blank range. You have enough talent, my dear fellow, soon to be acquainted with the horrible, unending battle which mediocrity wages against superiority. If one evening you lose twenty-five louis, the next day you will be accused of being a gambler and your best friends will say that the day before you lost twenty-five thousand francs. If you have a headache, you will be called a lunatic. If you have one outburst of temper, they will say you are a social misfit. If, in order to resist this army of pygmies, you muster your superior forces, your best friends will cry out that you want to eat up everything, that you claim to have the right to dominate and lord it over others. In short, your good qualities will become failings, your failings will become vices, and your virtues will be crimes. If you have saved a man, they'll say you have killed him; if your patient is in circulation again, they will affirm that you have sacrificed the future to the present; if he is not dead, he will die. Hesitate, and you will be lost! Invent anything at all, claim your just due, you will be regarded as a sly character, difficult to deal with, who is standing in the way of the young men. So, my dear fellow, if I don't believe in God, I believe still less in man. You recognize in me a Desplein very different from the Desplein everyone speaks ill of, don't you? But let's not rummage in this muck heap. Well, I used to live in this house; I was busy working to pass my first examination and I hadn't a sou. I had reached one of those extreme situations where, you know, a man says to himself, "I shall join the army." I had one last hope. I was expecting from home a trunk full of linen, a present from old aunts of the kind who, knowing nothing of Paris, think of your shirts and imagine that with thirty francs a month their nephew lives on caviar. The trunk arrived while I was at the school; the carriage cost forty francs. The porter, a German cobbler who lived in a garret, had paid the money and was keeping the trunk. I went for a walk in the Rue des Fossés-Saint-Germain-des-Prés and in the Rue de l'Ecole-de-Médecine, but I could not think up a plan which would deliver my trunk to me without my having to pay the forty francs; naturally I would have paid them after I had sold the linen. My stupidity made me realize that I was gifted for nothing but surgery. My dear fellow, sensitive souls whose gifts are deployed in a lofty sphere are lacking in that spirit of intrigue which is so resourceful in contriving schemes. *Their* genius lies in chance; they don't seek for things, they come on them by chance. Well, I returned at nightfall at the same time that my neighbour, a water-carrier named Bourgeat, a man from Saint-Flour, was going home. We knew each other in the way two tenants do who have rooms on the same landing, and who hear each other sleeping, coughing, and dressing, till in the end they get used to one another. My neighbour informed me that the landlord, to whom I owed three quarters' rent, had turned me out; I would have to clear out the next day. He himself had been given notice because of his calling. I spent the most unhappy night of my life. Where would I find a carrier to remove my poor household affairs and my books? How would I be able to pay the carrier and the porter? Where was I to go? I kept on asking myself these unanswerable questions through my tears, like a madman repeating a refrain. I fell asleep. Poverty has in its favour an exquisite sleep filled with beautiful dreams. The next morning, just as I was eating my bowlful of crumbled bread and milk, Bourgeat came in and said in his bad French, "*Monchieur l'étudiant*, I'm a poor man, a foundling from the Chain-Flour hospital. I've no father or mother and I'm not rich enough to get married. You haven't many relations either, or much in the way of hard cash. Now listen. I've got a hand-cart downstairs which I've hired for two *chous* an hour. It'll take all our things. If you're willing, we'll look for digs together since we're turned out of here. After all, this place isn't an earthly paradise."

"'I know that alright, Bourgeat, my good fellow," I

replied. "But I'm in rather a jam. Downstairs I have a trunk containing linen worth a hundred crowns. With that I could pay the landlord and what I owe the porter, but I haven't got a hundred sous."

'"That doesn't matter, I've got some cash," Bourgeat replied cheerfully, showing me a filthy old leather purse. "Keep your linen."

'Bourgeat paid my three quarters' rent and his own and settled with the porter. Then he put our furniture and my linen on to his cart and dragged it through the streets, stopping in front of every house which had a "to let" sign hanging out. My job was to go up and see if the place to let would suit us. At midday we were still wandering about the Latin Quarter without having found anything. The price was a great difficulty. Bourgeat suggested that we should have lunch at a wine-shop; we left our cart at the door. Towards evening, I discovered in the Cour de Rohan, Passage du Commerce, two rooms, separated by the stair in the attic at the top of a house. The rent was sixty francs a year each. We were housed at last, my humble friend and I. We had dinner together. Bourgeat, who earned about fifty sous a day, had about a hundred crowns. He was soon going to be able to realize his ambition and buy a water-cart and a horse. When he learned about my situation (for he dragged my secrets out of me with a deep cunning and a good nature the memory of which still touches my heart), he gave up for some time his whole life's ambition. Bourgeat had been a street-merchant for

21

twenty-two years; he sacrificed his hundred crowns to my future.'

Desplein gripped Bianchon's arm with emotion.

'He gave me the money I needed for my exams. My friend, that man realized that I had a mission, that the needs of my intelligence were more important than his own. He took care of me; he called me his child and lent me the money I needed to buy books. Sometimes he would come in very quietly to watch me working. Last but not least, he took care, as a mother might have done, to see that instead of the bad and insufficient food which I had been forced to put up with, I had a healthy and plentiful diet. Bourgeat, who was a man of about forty, had the face of a medieval burgess, a dome-like forehead and a head that a painter might have used as a model for Lycurgus. The poor man's heart was filled with affections which had no outlet. The only creature that had ever loved him was a poodle which had died a short time before. He talked to me continually about it and asked me if I thought that the Church would be willing to say Masses for the repose of its soul. His dog was, so he said, a true Christian and it had gone to church with him for twelve years, without ever barking there. It had listened to the organ without opening its mouth and squatted beside him with a look that made him think it was praying with him. This man transferred all his affections to me; he accepted me as a lonely and unhappy creature. He became for me the most attentive of mothers, the most tactful of benefactors, in short, the ideal of that virtue which delights in its own work. Whenever I met him in the street, he would glance at me with an understanding look filled with remarkable nobility; then he would pretend to walk as if he was carrying nothing. He seemed happy to see me in good health and well-dressed. In short, it was the devotion of a man of the people, the love of a working-girl transferred to a higher sphere. Bourgeat did my errands; he woke me up at night at the hours I asked him to. He cleaned my lamp and polished our landing. He was as good a servant as he was a father, and tidy as an English girl. He did the housework. Like Philopoemen he used to saw up our wood, doing everything with simplicity and dignity, for he seemed to realize that his objective added nobility to everything he did. When I left this good man to do my residence at the Hôtel Dieu, he felt an indescribable grief at the thought that he could no longer live with me. But he consoled himself with the prospect of saving up the money needed for the expenses of my thesis, and made me promise to come and see him on my days off. Bourgeat was proud of me; he loved me both for my sake and for his own. If you look up my thesis you will see that it was dedicated to him. During the last year of my internship, I had earned enough money to pay back everything I owed to this admirable Auvergnat, by buying him a horse and a water-cart. He was furious when he knew that I had been depriving myself of my money, and nevertheless he was delighted to see his wishes realized. He both laughed and scolded me. He looked at his cart and his horse, wiping a tear from his eyes as he said, "That's bad! Oh, what a splendid cart! You shouldn't have done it. The horse is as strong as an Auvergnat." I have never seen anything more moving than this scene. Bourgeat absolutely insisted on buying me that case of instruments mounted in silver which you have seen in my study, and which is for me the most valuable thing I have there. Although he was thrilled by my first successes, he never let slip the least word or gesture which implied, "That man's success is due to me." And yet, without him, poverty would have killed me. The poor man had dug his own grave to help me. He had eaten nothing but bread rubbed with garlic, so that I could have coffee to help me work at night. He fell ill. As you can imagine, I spent the nights at his bedside. I pulled him through the first time, but he had a relapse two years later, and in spite of the most constant care, in spite of the greatest efforts of medical science, his end had come. No king was ever as well cared for as he was. Yes, Bianchon, to snatch that life from death I made supreme efforts. I wanted to make him live long enough for me to show him the results of his work and realize all his hopes for me; I wanted to satisfy the only gratitude which has ever filled my heart and put out a fire which still burns me today.'

After a pause, Desplein, visibly moved, resumed his tale. 'Bourgeat, my second father, died in my arms leaving me everything he possessed in a will which he had had made by a public letter-writer and dated the year when we went to live in the Cour de Rohan. This man had the simple faith of a charcoal-burner. He loved the Blessed Virgin as he would have loved his wife. Although he was an ardent Catholic, he had never said a word to me about my lack of religion. When his life was in danger, he begged me to do everything possible to enable him to have the help of the Church. I had Mass said for him every day. Often, during the night, he would express fears for his future; he was afraid that he had not lived a sufficiently holy life. Poor man! He worked from morning to night. To whom then would Paradise belong – if there is a Paradise? He received the last rites like the saint he was and his death was worthy of his life. I was the only person to attend his funeral. When I had buried my only benefactor, I tried to think of a way of paying my debt to him. I realized that he had neither family nor friends, wife nor children. But he was a believer, he had a religious conviction. Had I any right to dispute it? He had spoken to me shyly about Masses said for the repose of the dead. He didn't want to impose this duty upon me, thinking that it would be like asking payment for his services. As soon as I could establish an endowment fund, I gave Saint-Sulpice the necessary amount to have four Masses said there a year. As the only thing I can give to Bourgeat is the satisfaction of his religious wishes, the day when this Mass is said at the beginning of each season, I say with the good faith of a doubter, "Oh God, if there is a sphere where, after their death, you place all those who have been perfect, think of good Bourgeat. And if there is anything for him to suffer, give me his sufferings so that he may enter more quickly into what is called Paradise." That, my dear fellow, is the most that a man with my opinions can allow himself. God must be a decent chap; he couldn't hold it against me. I swear to you, I would give my fortune to be a believer like Bourgeat.'

Bianchon, who looked after Desplein in his last illness, dares not affirm nowadays that the distinguished surgeon died an atheist. Believers will like to think that the humble Auvergnat will have opened the gate of heaven for him as, earlier, he had opened for him the gate of that earthly temple on whose doorway is written *Aux grands hommes la patrie reconnaissante.**

---

* These words (meaning 'To our great men from their grateful country') are inscribed above the doorway of the Panthéon in Paris where many of the great men of France are buried.

The Conscript

Sometimes they saw that, by a phenomenon of vision or movement, he could abolish space in its two aspects of Time and Distance, one of these being intellectual and the other physical.

Histoire Intellectuelle de Louis Lambert.

One evening in the month of November 1793, the most important people in Carentan were gathered together in the drawing-room of Madame de Dey, who received company every day. Certain circumstances, which would not have attracted attention in a large town but which were bound to arouse curiosity in a small one, gave an unwonted interest to this everyday gathering. Two days earlier, Madame de Dey had closed her doors to visitors, and she had not received any the previous day either, pretending that she was unwell. In normal times these two events would have had the same effect in Carentan as the closing of the theatres has in Paris. On such days existence is, in a way, incomplete. But in 1793 Madame de Dey's behaviour could have the most disastrous consequences. At that time if an aristocrat risked the least step, he was nearly always involved in a matter of life and death. To understand properly the eager curiosity and the narrow-minded cunning which, during that evening, were expressed on the faces of all these Norman worthies, but above all to appreciate the secret worries of Madame de Dey, the part she played at Carentan must be explained. As the critical position in which she was placed at that time was, no doubt, that of many people during the Revolution, the sympathies of more than one reader will give an emotional background to this narrative.

Madame de Dey, the widow of a lieutenant-general, a chevalier of several orders, had left the Court at the beginning of the emigration. As she owned a considerable amount of property in the Carentan region, she had taken refuge there, hoping that the influence of the Terror would be little felt in those parts. This calculation, founded on an accurate knowledge of the region, was correct. The Revolution wrought little havoc in Lower Normandy. Although, in the past, when Madame de Dey visited her property in Normandy, she associated only with the noble families of the district, she now made a policy of opening her doors to the principal townspeople and to the new authorities, trying to make them proud of having won her over, without arousing either their hatred or their jealousy. She was charming and kind, and gifted with that indescribable gentleness which enabled her to please without having to lower herself or ask favours. She had succeeded in winning general esteem thanks to her perfect tact which enabled her to keep wisely to a narrow path, satisfying the demands of that mixed society without humiliating the touchy *amour propre* of the parvenus, or upsetting the sensibilities of her old friends.

She was about thirty-eight years old, and she still retained, not the fresh, rounded good looks which distinguish the girls of Lower Normandy, but a slender, as it were aristocratic, type of beauty. Her features were neat and delicate; her figure was graceful and slender. When she spoke, her pale face seemed to light up and come to life. Her large black eyes were full of friendliness, but their calm, religious expression seemed to show that the mainspring of her existence was no longer within herself. In the prime of her youth she had been married to a jealous old soldier, and her false position at a flirtatious court no doubt helped to spread a veil of serious melancholy over a face which must once have shone with the charms and vivacity of love. Since, at an age when a woman still feels rather than reflects, she had always had to repress her instinctive feminine feelings and emotions, passion had remained unawakened in the depths of her heart. And so her principal attraction stemmed from this inner youthfulness which was, at times, revealed in her face and which gave her thoughts an expression of innocent desire. Her appearance commanded respect, but in her bearing and in her voice there was always the expectancy of an unknown future as with a young girl. Soon after meeting her the least susceptible of men would find himself in love with her and yet retain a kind of respectful fear of her, inspired by her courteous, dignified manner. Her soul, naturally great but strengthened by cruel struggles, seemed far removed from ordinary humanity, and men recognized their inferiority. This soul needed a dominating passion. Madame de Dey's affections were thus concentrated in one single feeling, that of maternity. The happiness and the satisfactions of which she had been deprived as a wife, she found instead in the intense love she had for her son. She loved him not only with the pure and profound devotion of a mother, but with the coquetry of a mistress and the jealousy of a wife. She was unhappy when he was away, and, anxious during his absence, she could never see enough of him and lived only through and for him. To make the reader appreciate the strength of this feeling, it will suffice to add that this son was not only Madame de Dey's only child, but also her last surviving relative, the one being on whom she could fasten the fears, the hopes and the joys of her life. The late Comte de Dey was the last of his family and she was the sole heiress of hers. Material motives and interests thus combined with the noblest needs of the soul to intensify in the countess's heart a feeling which is already so strong in women. It was only by taking the greatest of care that she had managed to bring up her son and this had made him even more dear to her. Twenty times the doctors told her she would lose him, but confident in her own hopes and instincts, she had the inexpressible joy of seeing him safely overcome the perils of childhood, and of marvelling at the improvement in his health, in spite of the doctors' verdict.

Due to her constant care, this son had grown up and developed into such a charming young man that at the age of twenty he was regarded as one of the most accomplished young courtiers at Versailles. Above all, thanks to a good fortune which does not crown the efforts of every mother, she was adored by her son; they understood each other in fraternal sympathy. If they had not already been linked by the ties of nature, they would instinctively have felt for each other that mutual friendship which one meets so rarely in life. At the age of eighteen the young count had been appointed a sub-lieutenant of dragoons and in obedience to the code of honour of the period he had followed the princes when they emigrated.

Madame de Dey, noble, rich and the mother of an *émigré*, thus could not conceal from herself the dangers of her cruel situation. As her only wish was to preserve her large fortune for her son, she had denied herself the happiness of going with him, and when she read the strict laws under which the Republic was confiscating every day the property of *émigrés* at Carentan, she congratulated herself on this act of courage. Was she not watching over her son's wealth at the risk of her life? Then, when she heard of the terrible executions decreed by the Convention, she slept peacefully in the knowledge that her only treasure was in safety, far from the danger of the scaffold. She was happy in the belief that she had done what was best to save both her son and her fortune. To this private thought she made the concessions demanded by those unhappy times, without compromising her feminine dignity or her aristocratic convictions, but hiding her sorrows with a cold secrecy. She had understood the difficulties which awaited her at Carentan. To come there and occupy the first place, wasn't that a way of defying the scaffold every day? But, supported by the courage of a mother, she knew how to win the affection of the poor by relieving all kinds of distress without distinction, and made herself indispensable to the rich by ministering to their pleasures. She entertained at her house the *procureur** of the commune, the mayor, the president of the district, the public prosecutor and even the judges of the revolutionary tribunal. The first four of these were unmarried and so they courted her, hoping to marry her either by making her afraid of the harm they could do her or by offering her their protection. The public prosecutor, who had been *procureur* at Caen and used to look after the countess's business interests, tried to make her love him, by behaving with devotion and generosity – a dangerous form of cunning! He was the most formidable of all the suitors. As she had formerly been a client of his, he was the only

* An official elected to represent the central government on local courts and administration.

one who had an intimate knowledge of the state of her considerable fortune. His passion was reinforced by all the desires of avarice and supported by an immense power, the power of life and death throughout the district. This man, who was still young, behaved with such an appearance of magnanimity that Madame de Dey had not yet been able to form an opinion of him. But, despising the danger which lay in vying in cunning with Normans, she made use of the inventive craftiness with which Nature has endowed women to play off these rivals against each other. By gaining time, she hoped to survive safe and sound to the end of the revolutionary troubles. At that period, the royalists who had stayed in France deluded themselves each day that the next day would see the end of the Revolution, and this conviction caused the ruin of many of them.

In spite of these difficulties, the countess had very skilfully maintained her independence until the day on which, with unaccountable imprudence, she took it into her head to close her door. The interest she aroused was so deep and genuine that the people who had come to her house that evening became extremely anxious when they learned that it was impossible for her to receive them. Then, with that frank curiosity which is engrained in provincial manners, they made inquiries about the misfortune, the sorrow, or the illness which Madame de Dey must be suffering from. An old servant named Brigitte answered these questions saying that her mistress had shut herself up in her room and wouldn't see anyone, not even the members of her own household. The almost cloister-like existence led by the inhabitants of a small town forms in them the habit of analysing and explaining the actions of others. This habit is naturally so invincible that after pitying Madame de Dey, and without knowing whether she was really happy or sad, everyone began to look for the causes of her sudden retreat.

'If she were ill,' said the first inquirer, 'she would have sent for the doctor. But the doctor spent the whole day at my house playing chess. He said to me jokingly that nowadays there is only one illness . . . and that unfortunately it is incurable.'

This jest was made with caution. Men and women, old men and girls then began to range over the vast field of conjectures. Each one thought he spied a secret, and this secret filled all their imaginations. The next day their suspicions had grown nastier. As life is lived in public in a small town, the women were the first to find out that Brigitte had bought more provisions than usual at the market. This fact could not be denied. Brigitte had been seen first thing in the morning in the market-square and – strange to relate – she had bought the only hare available. The whole town knew that Madame de Dey did not like game. The hare became a starting point for endless conjectures. As they took their daily walk, the old men noticed in the countess's house a kind of concentrated activity which was revealed by the very precautions taken by the servants to conceal it. The valet was beating a carpet in the garden. The previous day no one would have paid any attention to it, but this carpet became a piece of evidence in support of the fanciful tales which everyone was inventing. Each person had his own. The second day, when they heard that Madame de Dey said she was unwell, the leading inhabitants of Carentan gathered together in the evening at the mayor's brother's house. He was a retired merchant, married, honourable, generally respected, and the countess had a high regard for him. That evening all the suitors for the hand of the rich widow had a more or less probable tale to tell, and each one of them considered how to turn to his own profit the secret event which forced her to place herself in this compromising position. The public prosecutor imagined a whole drama in which Madame de Dey's son would be brought to her house at night. The mayor thought that a non-juring priest had arrived from La Vendée and sought asylum with her.* But the purchase of a hare on a Friday couldn't be explained by this story. The president of the district was convinced that she was hiding a chouan† or a Vendéen leader who was being hotly pursued. Others thought it was a noble who had escaped from the Paris

---

*   The priests often helped the inhabitants of La Vendée in the west of France in their risings against the Revolution.

†   The chouans were royalist insurgents from Western France who engaged in guerrilla warfare against the Revolution.

prisons. In short, everyone suspected the countess of being guilty of one of those acts of generosity which the laws of that period called a crime and which could lead to the scaffold. The public prosecutor, however, whispered that they must be silent and try to save the unfortunate woman from the abyss towards which she was hastening.

'If you make this affair known,' he added, 'I shall be obliged to intervene, to search her house, and then! . . .' He said no more but everyone understood what he meant.

The countess's real friends were so alarmed for her that, on the morning of the third day, the *procureur-syndic** of the commune got his wife to write her a note urging her to receive company that evening as usual. Bolder still, the retired merchant called at Madame de Dey's house during the morning. Very conscious of the service which he wanted to render her, he insisted on being allowed in to see her, and was amazed when he caught sight of her in the garden, busy cutting the last flowers from her borders to fill her vases.

'She must have given refuge to her lover,' the old man said to himself, as he was overcome with pity for this charming woman. The strange expression of the countess's face confirmed his suspicions. The merchant was deeply moved by this devotion which is so natural to

* See note 1 above.

women, but which men always find touching because they are all flattered by the sacrifices which a woman makes for a man; he told the countess about the rumours which were all over the town, and of the danger in which she was placed. 'For,' he said in conclusion, 'though some of our officials may be willing to forgive you for acting heroically to save a priest, nobody will pity you if they find out you are sacrificing yourself for the sake of a love affair.'

At these words, Madame de Dey looked at the old man with a distraught and crazy expression which made him shudder, despite his age.

'Come with me,' she said taking him by the hand and leading him into her room where, having first made sure that they were alone, she took a dirty crumpled letter from the bodice of her dress. 'Read that,' she cried pronouncing the words with great effort.

She collapsed into her chair, as if she were overcome. While the old merchant was looking for his glasses and cleaning them, she looked up at him, examined him for the first time with interest and said gently in a faltering voice, 'I can trust you.'

'Have I not come to share in your crime?' replied the worthy man simply.

She gave a start. For the first time in this little town, her soul felt sympathy with another's. The merchant understood at once both the dejection and the joy of the countess. Her son had taken part in the Granville expedition;[*] his letter to his mother was written from the depths of his prison, giving her one sad, yet joyful hope. He had no doubts about his means of escape, and he mentioned three days in the course of which he would come to her house, in disguise. The fatal letter contained heart-rending farewells in case he would not be at Carentan by the evening of the third day, and he begged his mother to give a fairly large sum of money to the messenger who, braving countless dangers, had undertaken to bring her this letter. The paper shook in the old man's hands.

'And this is the third day,' cried Madame de Dey as she got up quickly, took back the letter, and paced up and down the room.

'You have acted rashly,' said the merchant. 'Why did you have food bought in?'

'But he might arrive, dying with hunger, exhausted, and . . .' She said no more.

'I can count on my brother,' continued the old man, 'I will go and bring him over to your side.'

In this situation the merchant deployed again all the subtlety which he had formerly used in business and gave the countess prudent and wise advice. After they had

---

[*] Granville is a small town, south-west of Carentan, on the other side of the Cotentin peninsula. In 1793 the Vendéens tried unsuccessfully to capture it for the royalists.

agreed on what they both should say and do, the old man, on cleverly invented pretexts, went to the principal houses in Carentan. There he announced that he had just seen Madame de Dey, who would receive company that evening, although she was not very well. As he was a good match for the cunning Norman minds who, in every family, cross-examined him about the nature of the countess's illness, he managed to deceive nearly everybody who was interested in this mysterious affair. His first visit worked wonders. He told a gouty old lady that Madame de Dey had nearly died from an attack of stomach gout. The famous Doctor Tronchin had on a former, similar occasion advised her to lay on her chest the skin of a hare, which had been flayed alive, and to stay absolutely immobile in bed. The countess who, two days ago, had been in mortal danger, was now, after having punctiliously obeyed Tronchin's extraordinary instructions, well enough to receive visitors that evening. This tale had an enormous success, and the Carentan doctor, a secret royalist, added to the effect by the seriousness with which he discussed the remedy. Nevertheless, suspicions had taken root too strongly in the minds of some obstinate people, or of some doubters, to be entirely dissipated. So, that evening, Madame de Dey's visitors came eagerly, in good time, some to observe her face carefully, others out of friendship, most of them amazed at her recovery. They found the countess by the large fireplace in her drawing-room, which was almost as small as the other drawing-rooms in Carentan, for to avoid offending the narrow-minded ideas of her guests, she had denied herself the luxuries she had been used to and so had made no changes in her house. The floor of the reception room was not even polished. She left dingy old hangings on the walls, kept the local furniture, burnt tallow candles and followed the fashions of the place. She adopted provincial life, without shrinking from its most uncomfortable meannesses or its most disagreeable privations. But, as she knew that her guests would forgive her any lavishness conducive to their comfort, she left nothing undone which would minister to their personal pleasures. And so she always provided excellent dinners. She went as far as to feign meanness in order to please these calculating minds and she skilfully admitted to certain concessions to luxury, in order to give in gracefully. And so, about seven o'clock that evening, the best of Carentan's poor society was at Madame de Dey's house and formed a large circle around the hearth. The mistress of the house, supported in her trouble by the old merchant's sympathetic glances, endured with remarkable courage her guests' detailed questioning and their frivolous and stupid arguments. But at every knock on the door, and whenever there was a sound of footsteps in the street, she hid her violent emotion by raising questions of importance to the prosperity of the district. She started off lively discussions about the quality of the ciders and was so well supported by her confidant that the company almost forgot to spy on her, since the expression of her face was so natural and her self-possession so imperturbable. Nevertheless the public prosecutor and one of the judges of the revolutionary tribunal said little, watching carefully the least changes in her expression and, in spite of the noise, listening to every sound in the house. Every now and then they asked the countess awkward questions but she answered them with admirable presence of mind. A mother has so much courage! When Madame de Dey had arranged the card-players, and settled everyone at the tables to play boston or reversis or whist, she still lingered in quite a carefree manner to chat with some young people. She was playing her part like a consummate actress. She got someone to ask for lotto, pretended to be the only person who knew where the set was, and left the room.

'I feel stifled, my dear Brigitte,' she exclaimed as she wiped the tears springing from her eyes which shone with fever, grief and impatience. 'He is not coming,' she continued, as she went upstairs and looked round the bedroom. 'Here, I can breathe and live. Yet in a few more moments he will be here! For he is alive, of that I am sure. My heart tells me so. Don't you hear anything, Brigitte? Oh! I would give the rest of my life to know whether he is in prison or walking across the countryside. I wish I could stop thinking.'

She looked round the room again to see if everything was in order. A good fire was burning brightly in the grate, the shutters were tightly closed, the polished furniture was gleaming, the way the bed had been made showed that the countess had discussed the smallest details with Brigitte. Her hopes could be discerned in the fastidious care which had obviously been lavished on this room; in the scent of the flowers she had placed there could be sensed the gracious sweetness and the most chaste caresses of love. Only a mother could have anticipated a soldier's wants and made preparations which satisfied them so completely. A superb meal, choice wines, slippers, clean linen, in short everything that a weary traveller could need or desire was brought together so that he should lack for nothing, so that the delights of home should show him a mother's love.

'Brigitte,' cried the countess in a heart-rending voice as she went to place a chair at the table. It was as if she wanted to make her prayers come true, as if she wanted to add strength to her illusions.

'Ah, Madame, he will come. He is not far away – I am sure that he is alive and on his way. I put a key in the Bible and I kept it on my fingers while Cottin read the Gospel of St John . . . and, Madame, the key didn't turn.'

'Is that a reliable sign?' asked the countess.

'Oh, yes! Madame, it's well known. I would stake my soul he's still alive. God cannot be wrong.'

'I would love to see him, in spite of the danger he will be in when he gets here.'

'Poor Monsieur Auguste,' cried Brigitte, 'he must be on the way, on foot.'

'And there's the church clock striking eight,' exclaimed the countess in terror.

She was afraid that she had stayed longer than she should have done in this room where, as everything bore witness to her son's life, she could believe that he was still alive. She went downstairs but before going into the drawing-room, she paused for a moment under the pillars of the staircase, listening to hear if any sound disturbed the silent echoes of the town. She smiled at Brigitte's husband, who kept guard like a sentinel and seemed dazed with the effort of straining to hear the sounds of the night from the village square. She saw her son in everything and everywhere. She soon went back into the room, putting on an air of gaiety, and began to play lotto with some little girls. But every now and then she complained of not feeling well and sat down in her armchair by the fireplace.

That is how people and things were in Madame de Dey's house while on the road from Paris to Cherbourg a young man wearing a brown *carmagnole*, the obligatory dress of the period, was making his way to Carentan. When the conscription of August 1793 first came into force, there was little or no discipline. The needs of the moment were such that the Republic could not equip its soldiers immediately, and it was not uncommon to see the roads full of conscripts still wearing their civilian clothes. These young men reached their halting places ahead of their battalions, or lagged behind, for their progress depended on their ability to endure the fatigues of a long march. The traveller in question was some way ahead of a column of conscripts which was going to Cherbourg and which the mayor of Carentan was expecting from hour to hour, intending to billet the men on the inhabitants. The young man was marching with a heavy tread, but he was still walking steadily and his bearing suggested that he had long been familiar with the hardships of military life. Although the meadow-land around Carentan was lit up by the moon, he had noticed big white clouds threatening a snowfall over the countryside. The fear of being caught in a storm probably made him walk faster, for he was going at a pace ill-suited to his fatigue. On his back he had an almost empty rucksack, and in his hand was a boxwood stick cut from one of the high, thick hedges which this shrub forms around most of the estates of Lower Normandy. A moment after the solitary traveller had caught sight of the towers of Carentan silhouetted in the eerie moonlight, he entered the town. His step aroused the echoes of the silent, deserted streets and he had to ask a weaver who was still at work the way to the mayor's house. This official did not live far away and the conscript soon found himself in the shelter of the porch of the mayor's house. He applied for a billeting order and sat down on a stone seat to wait. But he had to appear before the mayor who had sent for him and he was subjected to a scrupulous cross-examination. The soldier was a young man of good appearance who seemed to belong to a good family. His demeanour indicated that he was of noble birth and his face expressed that intelligence which comes from a good education.

'What's your name?' asked the mayor looking at him knowingly.

'Julien Jussien,' replied the conscript.

'And where do you come from?' asked the official with an incredulous smile.

'From Paris.'

'Your comrades must be some distance away,' continued the Norman half jokingly.

'I am three miles ahead of the battalion.'

'Some special feeling attracts you to Carentan, no doubt, *citoyen réquisitionnaire*,'* said the mayor shrewdly.

'It is all right,' he added, as with a gesture he imposed silence on the young man who was about to speak. 'We know where to send you. There you are,' he added giving him his billeting order. 'Off you go, *citoyen Jussien.*'

There was a tinge of irony in the official's tone as he pronounced these last two words and handed out a billet order giving the address of Madame de Dey's house. The young man read the address with an air of curiosity.

'He knows quite well that he hasn't far to go. And once

* *Citoyen* was a form of address during the Revolution replacing *monsieur*. A decree passed by the National Convention in 1793 called for military service all men between eighteen and twenty-five. The conscripts were known as *réquisitionnaires*.

he's outside he'll soon be across the square,' exclaimed the mayor talking to himself as the young man went out. He's got some nerve! May God guide him! He has an answer to everything. Yes, but if anyone but me had asked to see his papers, he would have been lost.'

At this moment, the Carentan clocks had just struck half past nine. The torches were being lit in Madame de Dey's ante-chamber; the servants were helping their masters and mistresses to put on their clogs, their overcoats or their capes; the card-players had settled their accounts and they were all leaving together, according to the established custom in all little towns.

'It looks as if the prosecutor wants to stay,' said a lady, who noticed that this important personage was missing when, having exhausted all the formulae of leave-taking, they separated in the square to go to their respective homes.

In fact that terrible magistrate was alone with the countess who was waiting, trembling, till he chose to go.

After a long and rather frightening silence, he said at last, 'I am here to see that the laws of the Republic are obeyed . . .'

Madame de Dey shuddered.

'Have you nothing to reveal to me?' he asked.

'Nothing,' she replied, amazed.

'Ah, Madame,' cried the prosecutor sitting down beside her and changing his tone, 'at this moment, one word could send you or me to the scaffold. I have observed your character, your feelings, your ways too closely to share the mistake into which you managed to lead your guests this evening. I have no doubt at all that you are expecting your son.'

The countess made a gesture of denial, but she had grown pale and the muscles of her face had contracted under the necessity of assuming a false air of calmness.

'Well, receive him,' continued the magistrate of the Revolution, 'but don't let him stay under your roof after seven o'clock in the morning. At daybreak, tomorrow, I shall come to your house armed with a denunciation which I shall have drawn up . . .'

She looked at him with a dazed expression which would have melted the heart of a tiger.

He went on gently, 'I shall demonstrate the falsity of the denunciation by a minute search, and by the nature of my report you will be protected from all further suspicion. I shall speak of your patriotic gifts, of your civic devotion, and we shall all be saved.'

Madame de Dey was afraid of a trap. She stood there motionless but her face was burning and her tongue was frozen. The sound of the door-knocker rang through the house.

'Ah,' cried the terrified mother, falling on her knees. 'Save him, save him!'

'Yes, let us save him!' replied the public prosecutor, looking at her passionately, 'even at the cost of *our* lives.'

47

'I am lost,' she cried as the prosecutor politely helped her to rise.

'Ah! Madame,' he replied with a fine oratorical gesture, 'I want to owe you to nothing . . . but yourself.'

'Madame, he's –,' cried Brigitte thinking her mistress was alone.

At the sight of the public prosecutor, the old servant who had been flushed with joy, became pale and motionless.

'Who is it, Brigitte?' asked the magistrate gently, with a knowing expression.

'A conscript sent by the mayor to be put up here,' replied the servant showing the billet order.

'That's right,' said the prosecutor after reading the order. 'A battalion is due in the town tonight.' And he went out.

At that moment the countess needed so much to believe in the sincerity of her former lawyer that she could not entertain the slightest doubt of it. Quickly she went upstairs, though she scarcely had the strength to stand. Then she opened her bedroom door, saw her son, and fell half-dead into his arms. 'Oh, my child, my child,' she cried sobbing and covering him with wild kisses.

'Madame,' said the stranger.

'Oh! It's someone else,' she cried. She recoiled in horror and stood in front of the conscript, gazing at him with a haggard look.

'Oh, good God, what a strong resemblance!' said Brigitte.

There was silence for a moment and even the stranger shuddered at the sight of Madame de Dey.

She leaned for support on Brigitte's husband and felt the full extent of her grief; this first blow had almost killed her. 'Monsieur,' she said, 'I cannot bear to see you any longer; I hope you won't mind if my servants take my place and look after you.'

She went down to her own room half carried by Brigitte and her old manservant.

'What, Madame!' cried the housekeeper as she helped her mistress to sit down. 'Is that man going to sleep in Monsieur Auguste's bed, put on Monsieur Auguste's slippers and eat the *pâté* that I made for Monsieur Auguste? If I were to be sent to the guillotine, I . . .'

'Brigitte,' cried Madame de Dey.

Brigitte said no more.

'Be quiet, you chatterbox,' said her husband in a low voice. 'You'll be the death of Madame.'

At this moment, the conscript made a noise in his room as he sat down to table.

'I can't stay here,' exclaimed Madame de Dey. 'I shall go into the conservatory. From there I shall be able to hear better what's going on outside during the night.'

She was still wavering between the fear of having lost her son and the hope of seeing him come back. The silence of the night was horrible. When the conscript battalion came into town and each man had to seek out his lodgings, it was a terrible time for the countess. Her hopes were dashed at every footstep, at every sound; then soon the awful stillness of Nature returned. Towards morning, the countess had to go back to her own room. Brigitte, who was watching her mistress's movements, did not see her come out; she went into the room and there found the countess dead.

'She must have heard the conscript finishing dressing and walking about in Monsieur Auguste's room singing their damned *Marseillaise*, as if he were in a stable,' cried Brigitte. 'That will have killed her!'

The countess's death was caused by a more important feeling and, very likely, by a terrible vision. At the exact moment when Madame de Dey was dying in Carentan, her son was being shot in Le Morbihan. We can add this tragic fact to all the observations that have been made of sympathies which override the laws of space. Some learned recluses, in their curiosity, have collected this evidence in documents which will one day serve as a foundation for a new science – a science that has hitherto failed to produce its man of genius.